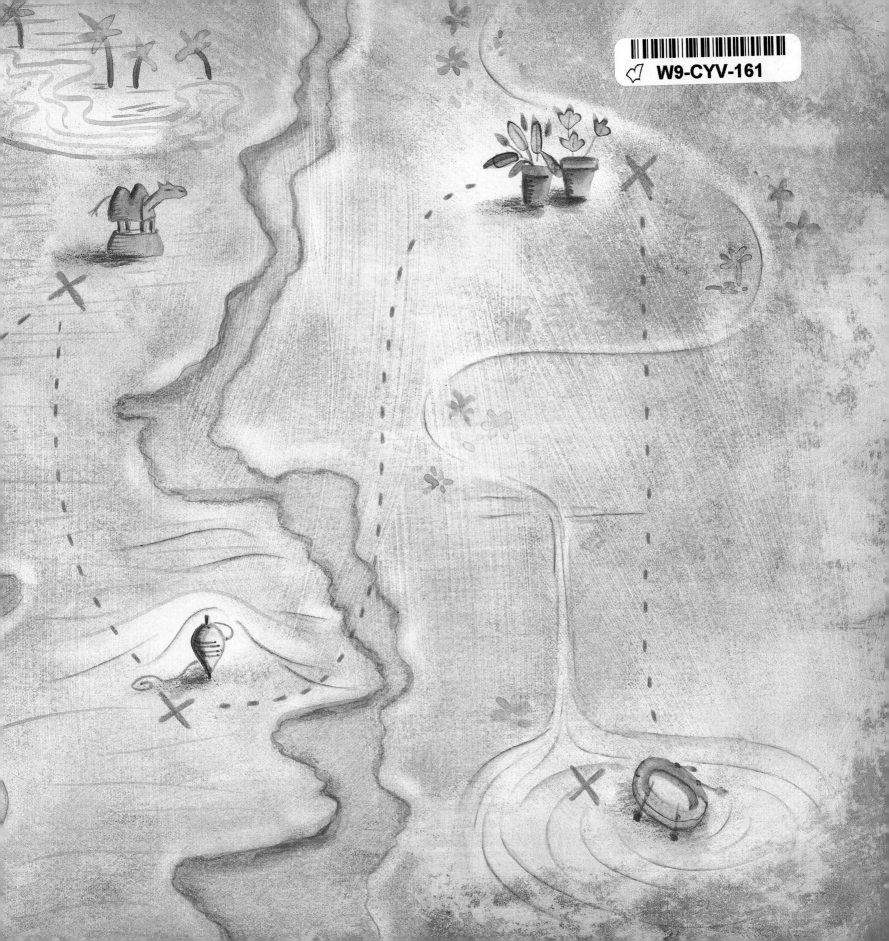

The Adventurers

Written by
Rachel Elliot

Illustrated by
Valeria Docampo

HUTTON
hg
GROVE

Outside, snow had
hidden all the footprints.
Inside, the fire was warm and bright.

The Velvet Cat curled up on the Blue Elephant's lap.
The Russian Doll leaned against the Pirate,
who wrapped his arms around her.
The Child sat on the back of the Rocking Horse.

"Let's go adventuring!" said the Child.

"We trek across snow-capped mountains,"
says the Blue Elephant. "I carry you through
the icy rivers on my back."

"I build an igloo!"
says the Child.

"I ride our sleigh through sparkling ravines!" says the Russian Doll.

4

"But we meet a Yeti!"
says the Velvet Cat.
"It imprisons us in its icicle cavern!"

Everyone shivers and shakes.

"I break the ice below us," says the Child.
"We drop down to the underground river
and sail away to the sea!"

5

"We sail the sea and rule the ocean waves," says the Pirate. "I fly the Jolly Roger and look for sunken treasure."

"I navigate by the twinkling stars," says the Rocking Horse.

"I swim with mermaids and dive for pearls," says the Child.

"But a sea serpent attacks
the ship!" says the Blue Elephant.
"It will swallow us whole!"

Everyone gulps and gasps.

"I call the birds to
help us!" says the Child.
"They carry the ship to
warm lands far away."

10

"We explore the sun-baked desert," says the Russian Doll. "I search for lost cities."

"I snooze in a silken tent," says the Pirate.

11

"I eat figs and drink
sweet milk,"
says the Velvet Cat.

"But a wicked genie traps us in a deep, dark, cave!" says the Rocking Horse. "We'll never see the sun again!"

Everyone quakes and quivers.

"I rub a magic lamp!" says the Child. "I wish to be on the other side of the world – somewhere hot!"

1

"We are jungle explorers!" says the Velvet Cat. "I leap from branch to branch and play with the monkeys."

"I build a campfire and sleep in a hammock," says the Pirate.

"We go rafting down the foaming rivers," says the Blue Elephant.

"But we plunge over a waterfall!" trembles the Russian Doll. "We will lose each other forever!"

Everyone holds on tight.

"Don't let go!" cries the Child.

The Adventurers tumbled together in a heap.

Outside, snow was still silently falling. Inside, the fire was glowing in the hearth.

The Velvet Cat curled up on the
Blue Elephant's lap. The Russian Doll
leaned against the Pirate, who folded
his dark cloak around her.

"Let's go adventuring again
tomorrow," said the Child.

And she yawned on the back
of the rocking horse,
and fell fast asleep.

22

For Rich, with love always x
R·E·

For Jean-Pascal Benet, an adventurer
who found love at the end of the world,
and became my brother
V·D·

The Adventurers
Text Copyright | Rachel Elliot
Illustration Copyright | Valeria Docampo
The rights of Rachel Elliot and Valeria Docampo to be named as
the author and illustrator of this work have been asserted by them
in accordance with the Copyright, Designs and Patents Act, 1988

Published in 2016 by Hutton Grove, an imprint of Bravo Ltd.
Sales and Enquiries:
Kuperard Publishers & Distributors
59 Hutton Grove, London, N12 8DS, United Kingdom
Tel: +44 (0)208 446 2440
Fax: +44 (0)208 446 2441
sales@kuperard.co.uk
www.kuperard.co.uk

Published by arrangement with Albury Books
Albury Court, Albury, Oxfordshire, OX9 2LP

ISBN 978-1-910925-19-5 (hardback)
ISBN 978-1-910925-18-8 (paperback)

A CIP catalogue record for this book is available from
the British Library
10 9 8 7 6 5 4 3
Printed in China

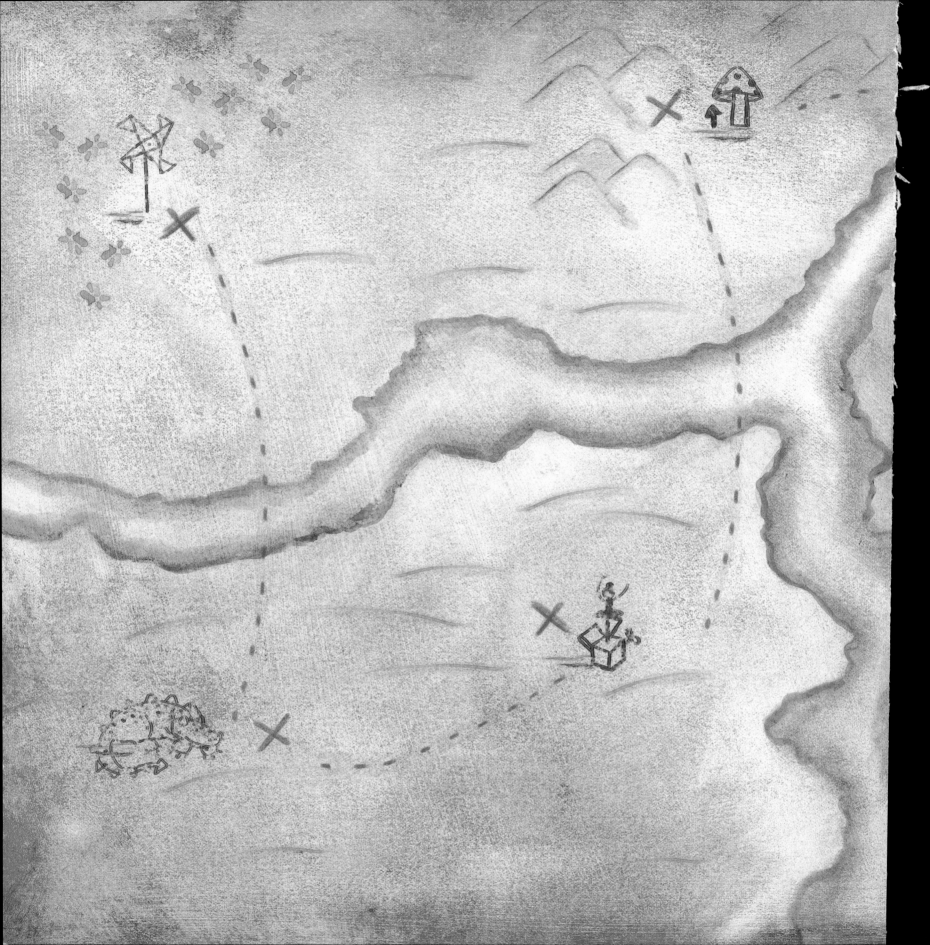